Rozelle Park:

Part 2:

The summons:

Chapter 1:

The Moonlight Beginning.

As the moonlit sky casts its luminous glow, Rozelle Park becomes the capturing stage where the magic unfolds. Acorn, the wise narrator, skilfully frames the scene, preparing us for the unfolding events of Part Two. Through Acorn's crystalline lens, we witness the tranquil coexistence with the harmonious that prevails in Rozelle Park, cradled with a gentle embrace of the moon.

Beneath the moonlit canopy, Rozelle Park thrives in a serene harmony. Creatures of all sizes exist, fostering a world of natural beauty. Towering trees stands tall, providing shelter for birds as they sit on their branches. Squirrels gather their acorns, while the rabbits gracefully hop through the grassy meadows. Butterflies and Moths dances among the flowers. In the tranquil sanctuary, each creature is a part of the delicate tapestry of life. There is a multitude of cohabitation that reflects the beauty of unity.

As the night progresses, Rozelle Park residents embark on their nocturnal journeys, to be associate with a shared purpose: to safeguard their beloved home. It is a world where the desire to intertwine within the moon's gentle embrace. In this moonlight haven, the story of Rozelle Park, Part two: "The Summons" is unfolding.

Major Tom, Nurse Glady's, and Peaches set out to locate his troops. As Robin returns from the Wee Loch, he immediately calls out, "Wait! I have got important news for you!"

Nurse Glady's warmly welcomes him with a greeting of, "Hello, Robin."

Surprisingly, Major Tom requests, "Did you manage to inform the Germans?"

Robin affirms that everything is well-intended. "The House Martins are now currently with the feelings of explaining the situation to the Germans."

Major Tom expresses his desire that the birds' assistance will not be necessary, his voice fills with emotion. He issues a series of orders, saying, "Robin, your mission is now over. I would like you to cross the Wee Loch, return to the Germans post, and inform the House Martins once they have finish conveying the message." He continues, "Nurse Glady's and I, will handle things from now on. I would like to sincerely request for the Germans to remain at their post and await for our arrival." Then he adds, "You and the House Martins can return to your nest and attend to your young ones and get some well-deserve rest."

Peaches, with her voice fills with anticipation, makes an inquiry, "Does this mean my mission is over?"

Major Tom, with a warm smile, confirms, "Yes, indeed Peaches. You have accomplished your mission. It's time for you return to your Dray and get some well-deserve rest."

Peaches is clearly exhausted yet relieved, she bellows, "I'm completely worn out. Take care, everyone. I'm off now."

Major Tom and Nurse Glady's bid farewell in unison, their voices tinges with gratitude, "Goodbye Peaches!"

As Peaches heads off towards her Dray, with her steps heavy with exhaustion, and Robin takes flight in the direction of the Germans, disappearing into the enveloping night. Peaches does not know that there is a secret yet to be revealed, lingering in the shadows of anticipation. Major Tom and Nurse Glady's set off to locate his men, driven by their unwavering commitment to this mission.

Barney's presence is distinguished by the unique sound of, "T' wit, T' woos." It is attribute with his large, luminous green eyes, and his ability to rotate his head 360 degrees, which's provides a guiding light for Rozelle Park. This design, which prevents the birds such as woody from colliding into the trees, but woody's unfortunate talent is evident. Once he has accidentally collided with an enormous window on a city skyscraper, cleverly designed to blend into the sky, posing a challenge for migrating birds to detect. Woody's survival from such an accident might be seen as unfortunate, or is it truly a stroke of luck?

Meanwhile, Peaches arrives at the old oak tree and finds Acorn engrossed in idle gossip, chatting about several topics without any particular focus. Hand, with a touch of nostalgia, catches sight of her and extends a greeting in the form a wave, his aged wood showing a silent warmth.

Peaches with a sense of accomplishment, informs Acorn. "I've finally passed on the message, to Major Tom."

Acorn responds with a wonder, "I'm glad to hear that. So, what's the plan?"

Peaches declares that "Major Tom has taken over the mission from now on, "with her quivering voice, and a tearful look in her eyes. She continues, "Robin and I will not be needed from now on. We can return to our daily lives, and the birds can continue with their nesting and raising their young." Then suddenly, Peaches adds emotionally, "I want to have babies, and I am not even pregnant yet."

Righty Face asks, with an excitement bubbling in his voice, "There's a surprise for you in your Dray?"

Peaches, with her curiosity piqued, eagerly questions, "What's surprise?"

Lefty Face chimes in, with the enthusiasm evident in his tone, "Go and look!... In your Dray!"

Peaches, with her heart racing of anticipation, repeats, "What surprise?"

Lefty Face insists with his playful urgency, "Go and look!"

Peaches dashes up the tree towards her Dray, with her heart fills of affection and excitement. As she reaches out for him, she discovers Doodle is peacefully asleep. With her heart races of love for him, her touch fills with tenderness, and she snuggles up, softly whispering, "Oh, Doodle!" Her love deepens in that precious moment, and she drifts off to sleep, envelopes in the warmth of their affections. The serene night beneath the stars becomes a cherished memory for Peaches, a testament to the profound romance that continues to blossom between them as they share their dreams and live their lives together.

Chapter 2:

The Hidden Telephone Network.

For the Old Oak Tree.

Returning to part one of this tale. Rozelle Park commences to unveil its enchanting magic as strange events unfold on a fateful night. As the Sun sets, an ethereal green light bathes the Wee Loch, forming an illuminating glow among the hidden statues and carvings in a mystical emerald mist.

This remarkable veil adorns Rozelle Park, providing it with a unique beauty, while safeguarding an age-old secret. The gates of Rozelle Park gently closes, revealing a profound truth to those who are fortunate enough to bear witness. It as though Rozelle Park itself holds a timeless secret, beckoning those present to embark on a journey where the boundaries between magic and reality blurred into one.

This captivating scene from Rozelle Park's history serves as a prelude to the mysteries that lie ahead, bringing readers deeper into a world where the boundaries of the ordinary and the extraordinary intertwine become a spellbinding way. Despite this enchantment, Woody, meticulously a crafted wooden Pigeon adorns with painted feathers, possesses the extraordinary ability to take flight.

Under the silvery moonlit sky, Woody springs to life. Rozelle Park's presence appears to be stimulating as he becomes a part of the night. His wooden frame dancing amongst the branches of Rozelle Park has elegance and style. Barney, the other carved bird, transforms Woody's nocturnal flights into a magical spectacle observed solely by the moon and the whispering trees, transforming them into a magical experience.

Lefty Face, one of the carvings, reflects on, "I don't think Barney is happy about Woody colliding into him."

Righty Face raises an eyebrow slightly and responds, "Certainly not! But he keeps rotating his head, making those T' wit, T' woos sounds."

Within the mystical park, an extraordinary electrical communication system resides within the Old Oak Tree, it activates a private line for discreet conversations. For public communications, the carvings can simply just speak out.

Lefty Face realises with a mix of fascination and temptation, "Woody, being a carve wooden pigeon, processes the ability to fly." Lefty Face adds, "Some reason, he has left his post!" And also, he adds, "But with a sense of duty reminds him, that he knows, he cannot stay away for long!" He adds with a hint of caution, "If he does, he's at risk of catching fire, and he must return quickly to his post."

Righty Face inquires with a mix of surprise and curiosity, "Does this means that Barney can fly?"

Lefty Face responds with a sense of wonder, "I suppose so! That Barney, can fly."

Righty Face raises his head and asks with anticipation, "Shall I tell him?"

With a mysterious expression etched on his face, Lefty Face ponders for a moment before uttering the words, "No , not yet?" He swiftly decides to reach out to Woody for answers, exclaiming, "Let me call on Woody and uncover what he knows!"

Lefty Face initiates contact with Woody by sending electrical impulse through his feet. Woody's left claw responds with a rhythmic tapping, tap-a tap, tap-a tap, conveying a friendly greeting of, "Hello."

With a sense of esteem and admiration, Lefty Face asserts, "I am sorry for disturbing you! But I speculate that you know." He pulses for a second, asks, "Who you are?"

Woody replies, "Yes, I'm a wood carving in the shape of a pigeon." And he also adds, "I call myself Woody, as it seems fitting to me."

Lefty Face remarks with curiosity, "So, you can fly?" and asks, "How did you leave your post?"

Woody joyfully explains; "Initially, I believed I was a real Wood Pigeon, carrying the memories of crashing into a window in the sky, but then I discovered my true nature as a wood carving, infused with his soul and memories."

Lefty Face solemnly states, "you cannot stay here. By tomorrow morning, you must return to your post!"

"I didn't know that, but I do know this, and I realise, I can't leave the park; unseen forces hold me back," Woody admits, his brows furrowing in frustration. "Why do I need to go back to my post?" he questions, his curiosity evident in his tilted head and his inquisitive tone.

Lefty Face takes a deep breath; determination filled his eyes as he begins to explain the instructions Woody must follow. "Woody," he starts, "You possess an incredible gift of flight, but remember, great powers, can carry a great responsibility." His voice maintains a gentle, and yet serious tone, underscoring the gravity of the situation. Lefty Face continues, his tone earnest, conveying his concerns. "I've already informed you that if you don't return, you'll ignite. Moreover, by 8 30 in the morning, when Rozelle Park reopens and the sun rises, your body needs to recharge. Only then, when Rozelle Park closes by 8 30 in the evening, will you be free to leave your post." His voice drops slightly as he adds, "There's something else you must know," with a tinge of sadness evident in his expression. "If your parent tree didn't inform you, daylight hours will shorten, reducing your recharging time. During the peak of winter, you'll enter in total hibernation until the spring. Hand will adjust the alarm on his pocket watch to account for this. Oh, and just one thing," he trembles slightly, "If you fail to return, the soul you've absorbed will be lost forever."

Woody responds with determination, "Thank you for letting me know, if I cannot stay here; Then I must go back to my post."

Lefty Face asserts, with his tone filled with urgency, "That's right. But before you go, you must make amends with Barney, or our lives will not be worth living. He will be moaning all night. Do not mention it to him, that you couldn't see him when you last had a collision with all the effort he puts in, for being a navigation beacon."

"I will do that," Woody answers with determinedly, he ends the call and immediately reaches out to contact Barney.

Barney feels the tingles of a sensation in his left claw and gives a series of taps, "Tap-a-Tap-a-Tap-Tap, and Tap," and he responds with, "T' wit, T' woos, T' wit, T' woos." He says, "Yes! Hello?"

Woody replies, as if his voice fills with a remorse, "Lefty Face told me to tell you that I'm deeply sorry for colliding into you." He continues, "I'm truly apologise."

Barney responds with a hint of irritation, "T' wit, T' woos, T' wit, T' woos." He says, "I have been working hard to prevent collisions for the protection of this tree, but you! managed to crash into me."

Woody inquiries, "What kind of owl are you?"

Barney declares, "A Barn owl."

Woody says, "My name is Woody and now I must head off, home." With that, he takes flight, bidding farewell, "Goodbye."

The Faces call out together, "Thank you, Woody!" With their faces beams with gratitude.

Barn owls are one of the most widely distributed species of owls in the world, found in all regions except the polar and desert areas. While they are nocturnal like most Owl species, in the UK and certain Pacific islands, they also hunt during the day. Barn owls have specially hunted for ground-dwelling animals. Their diet primarily consists of small mammals, which they locate by relying on their extremely acute hearing.

In general, Barn Owls forms lifelong partnerships, although if one pair dies, a new bond may be formed. Breeding occurs at various times of the year, and they typically nest in a hollow trees, old buildings, or on the cliff crevice. Breeding takes place only when there is an abundance of food available. Incubation is conducted solely by the females, and on average, they raise around four owlets,' depending on the Male to provide them with the food.

Chapter 3:

Robin Returns to say the mission is over.

The Martin's Departure

Robin finally arrives at the other side of the Wee Loch. He observes the House Martins engage in a conversation with the Germans, who are a bit bewildered by the war circumstances. Martin, the leader of the House Martins, tries to provide some clarity, stating, "We are in a park called Rozelle, somewhere in Scotland." As Robin alights gracefully on one of the wooden poppies. He adds to his presence to the scene, ready to continue the unfolding events.

"Hallo Dort!" Asks Robin and the House Martins says, "Hello." The German speaks in their own language saying, "Willkommen." Robin must pass on a message to the Germans, as instructed by Major Tom. He delivers the message in German, "Sie, sollen bleiben und auf Major Tom, Nurse Gladys und seine truppen warten," (They should stay and wait for Major Tom, Nurse Gladys, and his troops to arrive.) And he instructs the House Martins, "You can fly back to your nest as you are no longer needed. You can continue to raise your young for the rest of the season until they migrate."

"Dann für du. Ich voll weit für Major Tom, Nurse Gladys und Herr Truppen." (Then for you, I am fully aware of Major Tom, Nurse Gladys, and his troops.) Hauptmann Clink Response, while Sergeant Schultz thinks he is going mad, "Ich höre nichts, ich höre nichts. Ihr sprecht auch mit den Vögeln. Ich muss Verruckt!"

"Are we all finished?" Martin inquires, and Robin responds, "Yes. You can go home. Those are the orders from Major Tom." Tweety, with a cheerful smile on his beak exclaims, "Come on, birdies, let's all head home." The Housemartins gracefully fly back to their nests, eager to reunite with their families. Robin stays behind, wanting to ensure they fully comprehend the recent events in Rozelle Park. They are no longer soldiers; they have transformed into sculptures, their new wooden bodies infused with souls and memories.

Robin asks the Germans, his voice filled with a mix of curiosity and concern, "Habt ihr alle verstanden, was hie rim Rozelle Park passiet ist? Versteht ihr, Dass euer Krieg vor hundert Jahren zu Ende gegangen ist? Die Erinnerungen, die ihr aufgenommen habt, gehören nicht euch. Etwas Seltsames ist mit der Sonne passiert, als sie in die totale Finsternis ging. Und der smaragdgrüne Nebel hat den Rozelle Park Leben erweckt." (Have you all understood what as happen in Rozelle Park? Do you understand that your war has been over for a hundred years? The memories you have absorbed are not yours. Something strange happened to the sun when it went into total eclipse. The emerald, green mist formed, brought Rozelle Park to life.

Hauptmann Clink answers Robin, "Ja, Ja, meine Robin. Ich verstehe." (Yes, yes, my Robin. I understand.) And Sergeant Schultz continues to moan, "Ich kann es nicht glauben, ich kann es nicht glauben. Ich höre nichts. Nichts! Dass ich immer noch mit den Vögeln spreche. Ich werde verrückt!" (I cannot believe it; I cannot believe it, I hear nothing. Nothing! That I am still talking to the birds. I must be mad!)

"Ich muss jetzt gehen, ich habe kleine zu aufziehen. Tschüss." (I have got to go now, got little ones to raise. Cheerio.) Says Robin. And all the Germans Reply, "Tschüss, und wir warten auf Major Tom und seine Truppen." (Cheerio, and we will wait for Major Tom and his troops.)

Robin flies back to his darling Robina nest, finding the Hatchlings peacefully asleep. He feels an overwhelming sense of joy that the mission is finally over, allowing him to focus on raising his young ones and making plans for their migration. Meanwhile, the Germans patiently await for the arrival of Major Tom and his colleagues.

Chapter 4:

Major Tom's Revelation.

A Glimpse of the Unseen.

Flight Sergeant Mitchell is in a dire situation, his Spitfire taking on enemy fire. His heart races as he clings to the controls, with the Spitfire's engine sputtering and smoke billows from the battered plane. With unwavering determination, Flight Sergeant Mitchell maintains his grip on the joystick, a fierce battle to remain alive and triumph raging in him. However, the time is now fading away.

Meanwhile, Major Tom and Nurse Glady's take on their approach to his men. Sergeant Lee catches sight of them, a glimpse of surprise in his expression. "Hello, sir, and to you, Nurse. To what do we owe this unexpected pleasure?" he inquires.

Major Tom responds, concern in his voice, "Well men, do you think you can free yourselves from your post?"

Gunner Peterson answers anxiously, "No, we cannot, and we tried, sir."

"I suppose Peaches told you that you are sculptures from the old soldiers from a war in the past, and you have been carved out from old trees." And Nurse Glady's adds, "You have absorbed their lost souls and have their memories."

Gunner Peterson responds respectfully, "Yes Madame."

Major Tom elaborates, "You lose control capabilities when you want to detach yourself from your post. The whole thing the self-conscious plays on your mind. Once you start thinking you are a soldier, it becomes possible to move. But when you think of yourself as a part of the tree, then you cannot move! To overcome this, you need to believe you are the person you think you are... That's when you can leave your post."

The two soldiers begins to free themselves from their post. Gunner Peterson makes his first attempt to lift himself up from his stretcher, struggling. Meanwhile, Sergeant Lee persist on with a determine effort, he pushes himself. His feet go "Pop" and "Pop," and finally, he's free, leaving Gunner Peterson feeling a bit envious.

Gunner Peterson expresses his frustration, saying "I have tried, but it seems like I cannot do this!"

Nurse Glady's reassures him, her voice filled with empathy, "I had the same problem. It took me an hour or so, to set me free. If I can do this, so can you."

Gunner Peterson persevered, attempting one step at a time. Slowly, he rips himself from his stretcher and springs onto his feet, triumphantly exclaiming, "At last, I am free!"

Major Tom Provides crucial instructions to his men, which they must obey. "First, you will need to return your post by 8:30 a m. If you do not, you will ignite into flames, and your souls you have absorbed will be lost forever."

Major Tom explains more about how absorbing the sun's energy and must remain at their post, which will rejuvenate them. He states that the upcoming winter is approaching, Hands regulates the alarm on his pocket watch to compensate for the shorter daylight hours.

In mid-winter. When there is not enough daylight for them to charge up, they will go into total hibernation. Right now, I have given you instructions, for when Rozelle Park opens, and so on," he says.

Then, Major Tom addresses his men, "At the moment, I would like you to join me to locate the Germans, who we hope, they're on the opposite side of the Wee Loch."

"How many Germans are there?" Gunner Peterson questions. With a concern etched on his face.

Major Tom replies, has his brow furrows, "I think there are three of them." He looks at Nurse Glady's with a hint of worry and asks, "you do not have to come with us?"

Nurse Glady's responds with a warm glow, her voice tinged with a hint of loneliness, "That's perfectly fine, Major, darling. The company is always welcome; I'm stationed alone, and the solitude can be quite isolating at times."

Major Tom nods with gratitude, "All right, you are welcome to come along."

Major Tom Troops and Nurse Glady's set out to locate the Germans. Approximately, half an hour into their journey, they stumble upon a downed airplane. Painted in green and brown camouflage with an R.A.F insignia on the fuselage. As a soldier from the great war, Major Tom has never seen an aircraft like this one before, piquing with his curiosity.

Sergeant Lee jumps on the port wing, a mix of excitement and caution in his expression, as he hears something struggling inside.

Chapter 5:

Metamorphosis.

From Human Flesh to wood.

Flight Sergeant Mitchell welcomes the troops with a mixture of hope and desperation in his voice, saying, "Hello, Chaps. Could you lend me a hand getting out of this old kite? I've been trapped inside this cockpit for what feels like an eternity since I was shot down over France."

During World War Two, pilots with three stripes were often referred to as flying Sergeants. However, just after the Second World War, the Sergeants' pilots were gradually phased out, and nowadays, all pilot members in the R.A.F, are commissioned officers. Today, there's a saying that when you enlist in the R.A.F, you only send the officers to war.

The troops on the wing, curiously with a hint of relief in their eyes. Major Tom, his voice tinged with curiously, breaks the silence, "What can we do to help?"

Flight Sergeant Mitchell, his desperation masked by a glimmer of hope, replies, "My canopy is stuck. If you can break the glass in a way that lets me out, I'd be grateful."

Sergeant Lee steps forward, pretending to smash the glass with the butt of his rifle, creating the illusion of shattered glass. Flight Sergeant Mitchell, seizing the opportunity, quickly lifts himself out of the cockpit and leaps onto the wing, producing the sound of banging wood.

As Flight Sergeant Mitchell gazes back at his aircraft, he is astounded to see not himself but the outline of a wooden Spitfire. The troops watch with awe, unaware of the illusion unfolding before them. Simultaneously, an eerie transformation occurs as Flight Sergeant Mitchell's body, once human flesh, begins to morph into wood. His limbs creak and stiffen, creating an unsettling atmosphere. The sound of banging wood accompanies his every move, leaving the troops and Major Tom bewildered by this otherworldly occurrence.

Flight Sergeant Mitchell extents his gratitude to the troops, his voice filled with relief, "Thank you, chaps! I honestly thought I wouldn't escape from this cockpit, By the way, I'm Flight Sergeant Mitchell, and what are your names?" His hand instinctively moves to wipe the sweat from his forehead, but to his bewilderment, there's no trace perspiration at all, a stark reminder of his transformation into wood.

With a panic and confusion mounts as he continues, "What has happened to me? I distinctly remember being shot down, but my body has undergone this inexplicable change." His voice quivers with a mix of emotions, leaving him and the troops in a state of astonishment and uncertainty.

Major Tom replies calmly, "You are in the afterlife, and we are in a park somewhere in Scotland. I am Major Tom, and these are Nurse Glady's, Gunner Peterson, and Sergeant Lee." He changes the subject by asking, "We have not seen that type of aircraft! Is it a secret weapon?"

Flight Sergeant Mitchell responds with a touch of surprise, saying, "You haven't seen a Spitfire before? That's quite remarkable!"

The troops reply in unison, "No."

Flight Sergeant Mitchell adds, "This is a Spitfire Mark 5."

Nurse Glady's notices Flight Sergeant Mitchell's uniform, and it is clearly not from her era.

She asks, "What year is this?"

Flight Sergeant Mitchell replies, "1942! Why?"

Major Tom drops a bombshell, "I've got a surprise for you; this is 2023."

Flight Sergeant Mitchell's eyes, seems to be appeared in disbelief. "What! 2023? So, what happened? Is the war over? Who won? He asks, his voice tinged with hope and curiosity.

Sergeant Lee follows up, "We do not know the outcome of your war. Can you tell us what happen to ours? Why are you now fighting another?"

Flight Sergeant Mitchell proceeds to enlighten the troops, his tone filled with history and urgency. "The Allies won, with the Germans surrendering in November, signing the treaty of Versailles on June 28, 1919. Subsequently, the disarmament of Germany began." He explains. "Kaiser Wilhelm II abdicated, and Germany collapsed, becoming a republic. Tsar Nicholas II abdicated in March 1917 leading to the Bolsheviks taking over and the founding of the Soviet Union in October 1917."

Continuing, Flight Sergeant recounts, "The Tsar's family was executed by the Soviets on July 17, 1918." He then discusses Germany's post-war struggles, saying, "With a depression, high unemployment, hyperinflation, democracy has collapsed. Adolf Hitler seized power from President Paul von Hindenburg, who became Chancellor. He rebuilt the German Armed Forces in defiance of the Versailles treaty, aimed to reclaim German territory, annexed Austria, Czechoslovakia, and then his army invaded Poland in September 1939. Britain and France declared war against Germany, and it was a disaster. The Germans blitzkrieg most of Europe, leaving Britain to fight on her own." Flight Sergeant Mitchell recounts these pivotal moments from the past as the weight of history hangs on the air.

In Rozelle Park, the statues' memories are resurfacing with greater clarity, as if the passage of time is gradually revealing their forgotten memories.

With a mix of relief and pride, Flight Sergeant Mitchell continues, "But Britain had a stroke of luck. Thanks to our beloved Spitfires and Hurricanes, the R.A.F defeated the Luftwaffe in September 1940. Hitler and his henchmen opted to invade Stalin's Russia instead." He adds with a sense of limitation, "That's all I can tell you."

Nurse Glady's, her emotions in turmoil, responds with a sense of dread, "Oh, my God, it's happening again, but this time it's even worse!"

The Spitfire, a single-seated fighter aircraft, played a pivotal role for the Royal Air Force and the Royal Navy, as well as many other Allied countries during, and after World War Two. This iconic aircraft saw numerous variants, ranging from the Mark 1 to Mark 24. The Spitfire was initially designed by Supermarine and then later on, the company was taken over by Vickers, all based on the innovative designs of R.J. Mitchell.

Taking its maiden flight on March 5, 1936, at Eastleigh airport near Southampton, the Spitfire quickly evolved into a symbol of British aviation prowess. It was introduced into the first squadrons on April 4, 1938, just in time to face the challenges of the impending war.

The majority of Spitfires were equipped with Merlin engines, providing versatility in armament. These aircraft could carry either Four 20mm cannons and 0.5-inch Browning Machine guns. Typically, the 20mm cannons were positioned on the outer wings, while the 0.5-inch Browning occupied the inner wing positions. However, some Spitfires were configured with four 0.5-inch Browning guns.

The Spitfire Mark 24, powered by a Rolls-Royce Griffon engine, marked a later variant in the lineage and was eventually phased out by 1960. Throughout its storied history, the Spitfire remained a symbol of British innovation and courage in the face of adversity.

Chapter 6:

Unveiling Statues.

A Journey Towards the Germans.

In the opening of this chapter, Major Tom provides critical advice to Flight Sergeant Mitchell. The atmosphere is altered with tension as Flight Sergeant Mitchell utilises Major Tom's guidance. With each word, the weight of their mission increases, and the anticipation of what lies ahead lingers in the air.

Major Tom, his voice is steady but laden with urgency, declares, "I have a multitude of tasks for you to undertake, each instruction is crucial. We will discuss them, en route to the Germans." As they journey on, Major Tom explores the peculiar events that occurred in Rozelle Park.

Half an hour later, a remarkable development unfolds. Unbelievably, the statues exhibit signs of life once more. A soldier, with a fear and confusion, envisions himself firing a relentless machine gun. Simultaneously, a Tank with rhomboidal shape emerges, its tracks encircling and etching into wooden terrain. The soldier's perception shifts from reality to hallucination as they continue to fire upon the imaginary threat.

In this surreal moment, the boundaries of the tangible and the imagined intertwine create an atmosphere of dread. Major Tom and Flight Sergeant Mitchell are in the vicinity of the forces at play and the significance of these eerie occurrences as they journey deeper into the unknown.

"Sir! Behold, Gunner Lewis relentlessly firing his machine gun. While that Wee Tank ambles along the platform, changing direction at will, oscillating between forward and reverse." Flight Sergeant Mitchell observes with a mixture of amusement and bewilderment. Gunner Peterson, accompanied by laughter, cannot help but find the situation entertaining.

Major Tom, however, realises the gravity of the situation and declares urgently, "We must put an end to this." The peculiar and unpredictable behaviour of the tank and Gunner Lewis's ceaseless firing require immediate action, as their mission takes an even more surreal twist.

The Lewis Gun, initially conceived in the USA, but ultimately adopted and mass-produced in the UK during World War 1, featured distinctive characteristics such as a barrel cooling shroud and a top mounted Pan Magazine. Its service extended across the British Empire and persisted until the Korean war.

Major Tom, now recognising the issue with the enigmatic Wee Tank, comprehends the complexity of the situation. He is aware that the tank has a crew of eight, each inhabited by unique souls and split personalities. This revelation adds an intriguing layer of complexity to their mission, promising a captivating and challenging endeavour as they navigate the intricacies of this extraordinary situation.

"Rat-tat-a-tat---rat-a-tat." Gunner Lewis go on with his relentless noise echoes through the tense atmosphere, seeming to be endless. The Wee Tank follows suit, the driver shouts out the commands,

"To the left, Driver! Straight ahead, and open fire!" and the crew goes, "Rat-tat-a-tat---rat-a-tat." His orders continue, "Germans to the left, and fire!" The crew goes, "Boom---Boom." Then he shouts, "reload!" and he gives more commands, "Germans to the right, and fire!" then crew goes, "Boom---Boom, "And he shouts, "reload!" The loudness persists as the Wee Tank reaches its peak.

Amidst the chaos, Major Tom's voice cuts through the clamour, "Cease fire! I ordered you to cease fire!" Both the Wee Tank and Gunner Lewis finally heed the command and halt their barrage. Gunner Lewis inquires, "What can we do for you? Sir!"

Major Tom responds, firmly, "Put down your weapons, and the crew living inside the tank, get yourselves out that thing and come here." The situation takes a momentous turn as Major Tom takes control of the surreal encounter that poised to unravel by the mysteries conceals within the Wee Tank and its extraordinary crew.

"Sir! We can't come out!" Commander Jones exclaims, his voice fraught with anxiety. "We're trapped inside the Tank, and the door seems to be locked and it won't open." The crew, known as Wee Willy after the tank's designers, responds with palpable fear at the prospect of being stuck within the confines of the tank indefinitely. The situation takes an even more perplexing turn, leaving Major Tom and his team with enigmatic task of freeing the mysteries that surround them.

The Tank War machine, nicknamed Little Willy, was designed by William Tritton and Major Walter Gordon Wilson. It was manufactured by William Foster & Co of Lincoln and Metropolitan Carriage of Birmingham. The crew of eight included a Commander/brakes man, a driver, two gear men, and four Gunners. This tank was specifically designed to cross the wide and deep trenches that were common on the battlefields of the Western Front during the first World War.

Little Willy saw its first action on the morning of September 15, 1916, during the battle of Flers-Courcelette as part of the Somme Offensive. However, its true mass deployment occurred during the Battle of Cambrai in November 1917 when approximately 460 Mark 4 tanks were used. Unfortunately, this battle did not result in victory, mainly due to the rapid advance of the tanks without sufficient infantry support. Communication was challenging, relying on Pigeons being released from the tanks. By the time the messages reached the infantry, it was often too late for reinforcement, allowing the Germans to quickly regain lost ground. Now in this story, we will refer to the tank as "Wee Willy."

Major Tom makes inquiries about the troop's names, and they respond, "Sir, I'm Gunner Lewis." Wee Willy, carrying its crew of eight, "The commander, Sergeant Jones, the driver, Corporal Smith, Gear Men, Lance Corporal Andrews and Lance Corporal Thomas, Four Gunners, Gunner Stewart, Gunner Dow, Gunner Smythe and Gunner Brown, all stand ready. Sir!"

Major Tom, puzzled, asks, "A crew of eight?"

Wee Willy responds, "Yes, eight, Sir!"

Gunner Peterson, interrupts, "Are we, the Pals Regiment, Sir! Do our, Pals Regiments, always stick together?"

Major Tom answers, in an agreement, nods his head, "Indeed, in which we are, Peterson." Then he orders Gunner Lewis and Wee Willy, "I need you all, to come with me!"

It is the only way; they can detach themselves from their posts. Gunner Lewis goes "Pop." And " pop." Leaving his post and his Machine Gun behind. Wee Willy, with wooden tracks driven by the gear men turning the drive wheels, has Lance Corporal Thomas on the left and Lance Corporal Andrews on the right, turning the wheels unaware of the noise they create-a sound like rubbing wood, going "Rub-a.dub, rub-a.dub" on the chassis. Wee Willy moves towards Major Tom as he leaves the Platform.

The Pals Regiments were a distinct and fascinating phenomenon in the British Army during the first world war. These units were formed during the early stages of the war in response to the overwhelming demand for troops. The concept was simple but powerful: encourage local communities, friends, and coworkers to enlist together, serving side by side on the battlefield.

The idea behind the Pals battalions was to maintain morale and camaraderie by allowing men to fight alongside those they knew and trusted. This recruitment approach aimed to alleviate the fear and loneliness often experienced by soldiers in the trenches. It was thought that if you were facing the horrors of war, doing so with familiar faces would make the ordeal more bearable.

These battalions were typically raised in towns, cities, and regions across the United Kingdom. They were named after the locality or occupation of the men who joined them. For example, Accrington Pals, the Footballers' Battalion, and the Birmingham Pals. This naming serves a badge of pride, emphasising the close-knit nature of these units.

While the idea of Pals battalions fostered an intense sense of community and mutual support, it also had its downsides. Tragedy often struck when entire groups of friends and neighbours were wiped out in a single battle. This had a profound impact on communities back home, leaving them devastated.

The Pals battalions saw action some of the most brutal battles of the first World War, such as the Somme and Passchendaele. Their commitment and bravery in the face adversity became emblematic of the sacrifices made during the war.

Ultimately, the Pals Regiments represent both the best and worst aspects of the Great War. They exemplify the camaraderie and spirit of service that drove many to enlist, but they also bear witness to the tragic cost of a conflict that claimed the lives of so many young men who had embarked on this journey together.

Wee Willy's commander, Jones, firmly commands, "Halt! We're now arrived!" The tank turns towards Major Tom, awaiting for further instructions. "What are your orders? Sir!" Wee Willy inquires.

Major Tom addresses his men, saying, "Well, we will be marching towards the Germans."

Gunner Lewis, surprised, asks, "The Germans? Sir!"

Major Tom clarifies, "Yes, the Germans. The war has been over for many years. This is the year 2023!"

Wee Willy's crew, along with Gunner Lewis, erupts into cheers, shouting, "Hip---Hip---Hooray! Hip---Hip---Hooray!" They are relieved by the news of victory and eagerly await new orders from Major Tom.

Major Tom introduces his men to Flight Sergeant Mitchell and Nurse Glady's expressing their anticipation and excitement. He mentions, "Sergeant Lee and Gunner Peterson, you already know due to this Pals Regiment. You will all be joining us on this mission. I will explain the orders during our journey." Then he asks, "Does anyone know any songs?"

Wee Willy's crew responds enthusiastically, "Yes, Sir, we do. We know songs like 'It's a Long Way to Tipperary' and 'Pack Up Your Troubles in Your Old Kit Bag,'"

"Alright, men, carry on," Major Tom says, and the Troops begin to sing, their voices echoing in the crisp 2023 air.

During the First World War, the soldiers found solace and camaraderie in singing songs that resonates with hardships of the era. Some of the iconic tunes included "It's a Long way To Tipperary," "Pack Up Your Troubles in Your Old Kit Bag," and "Over There" by George M. Cohan. These songs provided a sense as a reminder of home. Music offers a brief escape from the horrors of the battlefield and became an integral part of the soldiers' lives during the Great War, offering comfort and a connection to their shared experiences.

Troops sings, in unison:

Pack up your troubles in your old kit bag,

And smile, smile, smile.

While you've a lucifer to light your fag,

Smile, boys, that's the style.

What's the use of worrying?

It never was worthwhile, so

Pack up your troubles in your old kit bag,

And smile, smile, smile.

Pack up your troubles in your old kit bag,

And smile, smile, smile.

While you've a lucifer to light your fag,

Smile, boys, that's the style.

What's the use of worrying?

It never was worthwhile, so

Pack up your troubles in your old kit bag,

And smile, smile, smile.

With the cheerful song echoing through the air, the troops, led by Major Tom, set off on the path towards the Germans, making their way around the Wee Loch. On the road, Major Tom begins explaining to the troops about the strange occurrences happening in Rozelle Park. They march forward, eager to hear more about the mysterious events unfolding around them in this year of 2023.

Chapter 7:

The Germans.

The Arrival of Major Tom's Troops.

In the heart of Rozelle Park, the Germans wait patiently, their emotions a mix with curiosity and trepidation. Anticipation fills the air, as they strain their ears, listening for the approaching footsteps of Major Tom's troops.

From a distance, the faint but unmistakable sound of singing carries on the breeze. The voices draw nearer and nearer, weaving a tapestry of camaraderie and hope. It's a melody that transcends the language, a song that speaks the yearning for connection and understanding.

As the troops draw closer along the track leading from the other side of the Wee Loch, emotions swell within each soldier. For Major Tom's men, it's a moment to highlight their resilience and their yearning for a peaceful outcome. For the Germans, it's a chance to observe the unknown, to step beyond the boundaries of their ways.

In this chapter, the convergence of these two groups in the moonlit embrace of Rozelle Park reveals the possibility of a new beginning, where shared humanity and a desire for understanding transcends the barriers that have been dividing them for too long.

Sergeant Schultz shouts in distress, his voice trembling with fear and confusion, "Ich werde verrückt, Ich werde verrückt!" (I'm going insane, I'm going insane.) in his emotional turmoil, he believes he is losing his sanity.

Lancer Schneider exclaims, "Jetzt spreche ich immer noch mit den Vögeln!" (Now, I'm still talking to the birds.) His words carry a sense of desperation as he admits that he still talking to the birds.

Revealing a deep sense of inner turmoil and confusion. Hauptmann Click responds, his tone filled with resignation, "O K. Alles klar. Ich spreche auch mit den Vögeln. Es ist etwas Merkwürdiges an diesem Ort." (O K. Alright. I'm also talking to the birds. There is something odd about this place.) His words convey a sense of acceptance as he admits to conversing with the birds and acknowledges the strange nature of their surroundings.

Sergeant Schultz, visibly annoyed, demands, "Woher kommt dieser Lärm?" (Where is that racket coming from?) His irritation is evident as he searches for the source of the disturbance.

Nurse Glady's sings:

Up to mighty London came,

An Irish lad one day,

All the streets were pathed in gold,

So, everyone was gay!

Singing songs of Piccadilly,

Strand and Leicester Square,

'Til Paddy got excited then,

He shouted to them there.

Troops sings:

It's a long way to Tipperary,

It's a long way to go,

It's a long way to Tipperary,

To the sweetest girl I know,

Farewell Leicester Square,

It's a long, long way to Tipperary,

But my heart's right there.

It's a long way to Tipperary,

It's a long way to go,

It's a long way to Tipperary,

To the sweetest girl I know,

Goodbye Piccadilly,

Farewell Leicester Square,

It's a long, long way to Tipperary,

But my heart's right there

Nurse Glady's sings:

Paddy wrote a letter,

To his Molly O,

Saying, "Should you receive it,

Write and let me know!

If I make a mistake in spelling Molly dear," said he,

"Remember it's the pen, that's bad,

Don't lay the blame on me."

Troops sings:

It's a long way to Tipperary,

It's a long way to go,

It's a long way to Tipperary,

To the sweetest girl I know.

Goodbye Piccadilly,

Farewell Leicester Square,

It's a long, long to way to Tipperary,

But my heart's right there,

It's a long way to go,

It's a long way to Tipperary,

To the sweetest girl I know,

Goodbye Piccadilly,

Farewell Leicester Square,

It's a long, long way a Tipperary,

But my heart's right there.

As soon as Major Tom and his men arrives, the atmosphere crackles with anticipation. Major Tom's voice rings out, sharp and commanding, as he shouts, "Parade, halt!" The troops responds with precision, their right feet stamping the ground in unison. Wee Willy, under the guidance of Commander Jones, come to a stop with a screech of brakes, a faint smell of smoke lingering in the air.

Major Tom's orders continue, and the troops execute each command with discipline. "Left turn," he commands, and the soldiers pivot gracefully to the left, their right feet hitting the ground in perfect unison. Wee Willy's gear men act in harmony, one turning the cog wheel forward, while the other keeps his cog wheel still.

"Stand easy," Major Tom ordered, and the troops relax, their right feet moving apart as they catch their breath. Wee Willy, a mechanical behemoth, remains still awaiting further commands.

Finally, Major Tom concludes, "Dismiss, "and the troops take a well-deserved break, sitting down on the ground to relax. Yet, Wee Willy remains poised, a silent sentinel in the midst of the moment.

Major Tom extends a warm greeting, saying, "Hi, I believe you've been waiting for us to arrive!" Hauptmann Clink responds with a respectful, "Ja, Ja, voll, welcome."

Major Tom proceeds to introduce himself and his troops with a sense of camaraderie, "I'm Major Tom, and here is my troops: Flight Sergeant Mitchell, who hails from a different era, Nurse Glady's, Sergeant Lee, Gunner Peterson, Gunner Lewis and our tank crew, known as Wee Willy." They all have offered a greeting with a chorus of "Hi."

Major Tom then turns to Hauptmann Clink; extending the invitation, "Could you introduce yourself and your men, Captain?" The air is filled with a sense of curiosity and a desire to bridge the gap between the two groups.

"Ja, Ja, voll, Major Tom. Mein Name ist nicht Hauptmann Clink, das ist Sergeant Schultz und Lancer Schnieder," Response Hauptmann Clink.

Major Tom proceeds to explain Wee Willy's unique nature, saying, "You see, Wee Willy used to be an armoured tank with a crew of eight. Don't be fooled. He is well and talks to himself, just say hello and you'll see what I mean."

Lancer Schneider greets Wee Willy with a friendly, "Hallo. Klein Willy."

Wee Willy responds with a mix of greetings, highlighting his diverse accents, "Hello, hi, Good to see you. You're welcome. Good day, sport, hi, to you all, what's up." The variety of accents adds an amusing and friendly touch to the encounter, breaking the ice and fostering a sense of camaraderie between two groups.

"Oh Lieber Gott: Oh Lieber Gott, Ist das die jenseits. Sind wir tot." Questions Sergeant Schultz.

Nurse Glady's notices something and remarks, "I'm not sure. I do think that I can understand German. He's saying,' Is this the afterlife?' After all, we do have a frame that absorbs the souls from the past."

Major Tom then asks the Germans, "Did the little birds explain everything to you?" The air filled with curiosity as both sides seek to comprehend the unique circumstances, they find themselves in.

As the Germans Soldier speaks, there's a palpable sense of tension in the air. He explains, "Jaa, they did. We can leave our post at 8:30 p.m., but must return by 8:30 a.m. If we do not, we will go up in flames, and the souls we carry will disappear forever." Hauptmann Clink wears a worried expression, clearly troubled by the gravity of the situation.

Nurse Glady's begins to grasp the German language, and her face shows signs of comprehension. Major Tom, who initially spoke in English, now communicates with the Germans seamlessly in their own language, and they respond in kind. This remarkable exchange leaves Nurse Glady's in awe. She then addresses Hauptmann Clink, saying, "Your English is good, Hauptmann."

To which Hauptmann Clink replies, "English! No, we are speaking German, and you're talking to us in German." Flight Sergeant Mitchell chimes in, adding with a hint of humour, "Sounds like English to me."

The dynamics of the conversation take a profound turn as language barriers appear to dissolve, leaving both sides perplexed. Yet, intrigued by the strange circumstances that have brought them together.

Since the day when the strange occurrence began, Rozelle Park has been working on deciphering and translating the various languages spoken within its mystical boundaries. This development promises to enhance communication and foster a deeper understanding among its diverse inhabitants.

Major Tom remarks, "Talking about establishing communications around here." And goes on to say, "somehow Rozelle Park has worked out all of this out!" He adds, "There must be some spirits at work, deciphering our languages and translating for us as we speak."

This newfound ability to communicate in one's own language marks a significant turning point in the encounters within Rozelle Park, allowing its residents to bridge gaps and share their stories and experiences more effectively.

Hauptmann Clink responds, "Is that so?"

As Major Tom questions him, "Are you speaking in German?"

"Yes," Replied Hauptmann Clink.

Major Tom challenges him with, "I'm speaking to you in English." Then he also adds, "There you go!"

Poor old Sergeant Schultz grows increasingly nervous in his afterlife, muttering, "I hear nothing! I hear nothing! The Englishman is speaking German."

The entire crew of Wee Willy shouts reassuringly, "Okay, Sergeant, you're hearing correctly, and you're not losing your mind. You're talking to the birds, after all; this is the afterlife."

Sergeant Schultz teeters on the verge of breaking down, exclaiming, "I must be going mad! Now I'm talking to the Tank!" He questions the crew, "How many of you are inside that thing?"

Wee Willy, with Gunner Smythe, responds, "What's up?" Gunner Brown adds, "Good day, sport." Gunner Smythe and Gunner Brown in unison, "Eight!"

Sergeant Schultz raises his voice in frustration, "What's up? What do you mean, 'what's up'? An Australian and an American voice inside that thing!"

The crew of Wee Willy laughs, saying, "Okay, Sergeant, calm down."

Sergeant Jones, the Commander of Wee Willy's crew turns to Major Tom with a mix of concern and eagerness. He asks, "Major, have our duties been completed, Sir?" He continues, emphasizing the lack of tasks at hand, "There seems to be nothing left for us to do here, Sir!"

Major Tom agrees, "You're dismissed."

Sergeant Jones, the Commander of Wee Willy, responds, "Thank you, Sir." Then he issues orders to the crew, "Driver, start the Tank up, and gear men, put her in reverse!"

The gear men reply, "Yes, Commander." Reverse is selected.

"Driver, please move on," orders Sergeant Jones.

With Wee Willy now in reverse and the left gear man turning his cog backward while the right gear man's cog remains still, Wee Willy backs up and turn right. The gear men select the forwards gears, and Sergeant Jones instructs the driver, "Driver, move forward."

"Yes, Commander," Corporal Smith replies.

As Wee Willy returns to his post, his crew starts singing, playfully mimicking the sound of gunfire. It seems like they're finding a way to keep themselves entertained during this downtime.

Germans to the left,

Germans to the right,

And Fire!

Rat-a-tat-a-tat,

Rat-a-tat-a-tat,

Boom, Boom,

Boom, Boom,

And reload!

Germans to the left,

Germans to the right,

And Fire!

Rat-a-tat-a-tat,

Rat-a-tat-a-tat,

Boom, Boom,

Boom, Boom,

And reload!

Chapter 8:

Poppies.

Symbols of Remembrance and the Changes.

As Wee Willy continues to repeat her marching song all the way back to its post, Sergeant Mitchell sits by the wooden poppies, addressing the men around him. "You see, old chaps," he begins, "I can explain how all these poppies came about." He goes on to clarify, "The poppies are the symbols for the fallen and the missing from the wars." And emphasises, "I'm telling you, Germans, the Great War is over, and you lost." He adds firmly, "The Allies emerged victorious! You Germans, surrendered on the day of November 11th, 1918."

Lancer Schneider acknowledges, saying, "I can see that we have lost." He then inquires, "What is your war, all about?"

Flight Sergeant Mitchell replies, "I'll explain, one step at the time. The poppies, after the Great War ended, were introduced by several nations as symbols of remembrance." He proceeds with his story, "In America, A teacher Miona Michael distributes silk poppies to raise money for a charity benefiting war veterans. In France, War-Widow Anna Guerin began producing fabric poppies for sale to aid those, affected by the war. He continues with his narrative, "Poppies became a symbol to remember those who perished and find a means to raise funds to support those who survived. The Red Poppy, in particular, remains an emblem of remembrance for the soldiers who lost their lives." He adds, "For others, its meaning has evolved in a response to contemporary events." He continues, "Now, in Britain, poppies are used to remember all the victims of active service in all wars since the Great War."

Flight Sergeant Mitchell begins to explain the origins of his war. He recounts how the Kaiser abdicated and was exiled to Holland, while Hitler rose to power in Germany, annexing Austria, and Czechoslovakia, invading Poland. He mentions the Tsar of Russia abdicating and his family being murdered by the Communists, with Stalin coming into Power. Due to Germany's invasion of Poland, he explains that Britain and France declared war on Germany.

Hauptmann Clink, in shock, exclaims, "When will these wars ever end?" He continues, "If the human race continues like this, there's no chance of survival at all. Are we heading towards annihilation?"

Major Tom, unable to provide an answer to Hauptmann Clink's statement, says, "Right, lads, it's getting late. We must allow the Germans to return to posts and regenerate, and we do the same." He orders his troops, "So, stand to attention, fall on parade, and form columns and ranks!"

Sergeant Lee takes charge and shouts loudly, "You heard the Major. Move!" Major Tom's troops align themselves into columns and ranks.

Major Tom issues commands shouting, "Parade, attention!" The troops snap to attention and stamp their feet resoundingly. He then commands, "Right turn!" The troops execute a right turn, their right feet swinging around and stamping with a resounding thud. He follows up with, "By the right, quick march!"

The troops step with their right foot forward, beginning to march while singing their marching songs, this time singing "Goodbye-ee."

Nurse Glady's sings:

Brother Bertie went away,

To do his bit the other day,

With a smile on his lips,

And his Lieutenant's Pips,

Upon his shoulder, bright and gay,

As the train moved out, he said,

Then he Wagged his paw,

And went away to war,

Shouting out these pathetic words:

Troops sings:

Goodbye-ee! Goodbye-ee!

Wipe the tear, baby dear, from your eye-ee,

Through it's hard to part I know, (I know),

I'll be tickled to death to go!

Don't cry-ee, don't sign-ee,

Bonsoir old thing, Cheerio, chin-chin:

Nurse Glady's sings:

At the concert down at Kew,

The Convalescents, dressed in blue,

Had to hear Lady Lee,

Who had turned eighty-three,

Sing the old, old songs she knew,

Then she made a speech and said,

"I look upon you boys with pride,

And for what you have done,

I'm going to kiss each one!"

Then they all grabbed their sticks and cried:

Troops sings

Goodbye-ee! Goodbye-ee,

Wipe your tear, baby dear, from your eye-ee,

Through it's hard to past I know (I know),

I'll be tickled to death to go!

Don't cry-ee, don't sigh-ee,

There's a silver lining in the sky-ee,

Bonsoir old thing, Cheerio, chin-chin,

Nah-poo, toodle-oo, goodbye-ee:

Nurse Glady's sings

Little Private Patrick Shaw,

He was a prisoner of war,

Until a Hun with a gun,

Called him "Pig Dog" for fun,

Then Paddy punched him on the jaw!

Right across the barbed wire fence,

The Germans dropped, in fear, dear oh dear!

All the wire gave way,

And Paddy yelled "hooray!"

As he ran for the Dutch frontier!

All the Troops.

Goodbye-ee! Goodbye-ee!

Wipe the tear, baby dear, from your eye-ee,

Through it's hard to part, I Know (I know),

I'll be tickled to death to go,

Don't cry-ee, don't sigh-ee,

There's a silver lining in the sky-ee,

Bonsoir thing, cheerio, chin-chin.

Nah-poo, toodle-oo, goodbye-ee:

As Major Tom and his troops march back to their posts and their voices gradually grow fainter continue singing all the way to the other side of the Wee Loch.

Hauptmann Clink brings up a point, saying, "I suppose we should return to our post."

Lancer Schnieder agrees with a respectful, "Yes, Sir." He then adds, "Sergeant Schultz always seems to find something to complain about."

Sergeant Schultz comments, "We will not, live to see Christmas again?" Seems to reflect a sense of uncertainty and the challenging circumstances they are facing.

Hauptmann Clink agrees, "You're right, Schultz. But we will plan for this before hibernation." He determine to plan something before that time, shows an initiative-taking attitude and desire to make the most of their current situation. It's important to find moments of joy and connection, even in these challenging times.

Sergeant Schultz, visibly frustrated, voices his discontent, "I don't like this! Curse this afterlife. I don't like any of it!"

It seems Sergeant Schultz has quite a knack for complaining. The Germans return to their post, and it's approaching 8:30 am. Hands watch alarm goes off, signalling the start of the recharge cycle.

Chapter 9:

Unexpected Encounters.

In the Moonlit Park.

A few hours earlier in the evening, Woody was returning from the Old Oak Tree, just before he approaches the Hazell tree. His keen eyes captured something glimmering on the ground, a shiny and sparkly object. With curiosity, he decides to land near it. As he examines the ground, he discovers a bright red ruby stone in a heart, a symbol of love, surrounded by a cluster of diamonds, all mounted on top of a golden ring. Woody delicately picked up the ring using his beak and carefully slides it onto the inside of his left wing.

"I love the look of this. I'll keep the ring and hide it in Doodle's Dray." Woody muses, admiring the exquisite jewellery. Lost in the beauty of the ring, he didn't notice a Fox silently approaches from his den nearby. Suddenly, the Fox pounces on him.

Startled and anxious, Woody exclaims, "What are you doing! You can't eat me; I'm made of wood."

Edward, the wooden Fox, grips Woody and replies with hunger in his belly, "I love the taste of Pigeon. It's my favourite meat, I'm going to eat you."

With a swift motion, Edward forces Woody to the ground, causing him to drop the ring, which fell close by. Edward attempted to bite Woody in the neck, but his wooden teeth nearly snapped in the process.

Frustrated, Edward mutters, "What the hell? There's no meat on this Pigeon."

"I've been trying to tell you. I'm a wood carving." Woody declares, still bewildered, and then asks, "Who are you?"

Edward glares at Woody, his sharp wooden eyes narrowing in confusion, He notices that the feathers on Woody start to disappear, transforming into a brownish wooden hue. He also watches as the furs on his red coat begin to vanish. Edward have managed to detach himself from the den, a large hole under his parent tree, by the time he pounces on Woody.

Woody, still bewildered, manages to ask, "What the last thing you can remember?"

Edward's hunger is now replaced by uncertainty, he says, "The last thing I can recall, I was out hunting, spotted a Pigeon on the ground feeding. I love the taste of the meat, this always melts in my mouth, delicious." He asserts, "I was, gradually sneaking up behind the Pigeon, and get ready to pounce." He continues, "The Pigeon escape from the noises coming from the hounds and found myself being chased by them. And, In the distance, there were sounds of horns blaring, and that was that."

Woody explains with his voice tinge with understanding, "That's the last memory your lost soul holds." He adds, "I'm Woody. And what should I call you?"

Edward responds, his wooden eyes betraying with a mix of confusion acceptance, "Edward."

Woody observes that Edward has managed to free himself from his post and remarks, "You've transformed into a wood carving and becoming a part of this tree. You must adhere to these rules and return to your post by 8:30 in the morning, or you risk going up in flames."

Woody attempts to elucidate the peculiar limitations and freedoms imposed upon him due to the mysterious events have unfolded in Rozelle Park, due to the sun's disappearance below the horizon during a rare solar eclipse.

Now, let's delve into the life of a fox. Foxes, these cunning creatures, are skilled hunters and are categorised as omnivores, much like humans. They hunt rabbits, birds, and diligently hunt for fruits and berries. In the wild, their average lifespan is between 3 to 4 years, whereas in captivity, they can live up to 10 to 14 years, similar to faithful canine companions. A female fox, known as a vixen, experiences pregnancy during the winter months, with her gestation period ranging from 40 to 60 days. While anticipating, she meticulously prepares a burrow in which she will give birth to her cubs, sometimes affectionately called kits or pups, typically numbers from 3 to 5.

After 4 weeks, the fox cubs cautiously begin to explore beyond their den. They don't wander too far, instinctively heeding their surroundings. During this time, they initiate their foraging expeditions and hone their hunting skills, targeting insects and worms. Around 12 weeks later, these young foxes have grown sufficiently self-reliant to leave the den and embark on their own journeys, perpetuating the timeless cycle of a fox's life.

Chapter 10:

Echoes of Connection.

Meeting Acorn and Unveiling E.S.P.

"So, this is the afterlife?" Edward asks, with his voice tingling with a mix of curiosity and apprehension.

Woody nods solely, with his eyes filled with the reassurance. "Yes, I'm afraid so." Has his voice carried the weight of the unknown.

Edward's emotions surges as he realises, "This means, I am not going to hunt for food for myself from now on!" With the relief that washes over him.

Woody reassures him, "Yes, the parent tree, where we've been living will provide the nutrients we need."

Woody begins to explain the telephone system with a sense of purpose. When you return to your den, if you think of a contact, one of your back paws will begin to tingle, then you will start to tap. You must think of something, absolutely anything you can think off." He emphasises, "I'll return back to my perch, and I'll give you a call. You don't need to speak; your mind will answer." Before he heads back, Woody retrieves a ring he had discovered. He goes to Doodles Dray, hides the ring, and then return to his perch. Meanwhile Edward also return to his den. He's only just settled down when of his back paws starts to tingle, tap-a-tap, and-tap. In his mind, Edward says, "Hello!"

Woody replies, "There you go. It's easy; now you're talking to me without moving your lips."

"Oh, I see. Who else will I need to talk to? I don't know anyone around here!" Edward admits with the uncertainty of his voice.

Woody explains, "There's another parent tree, just like this one and everybody calls it, The Old Oak Tree." He adds, "That there is a face that is carved out and he is called Acorn, and you can call him. All you need to do is think Acorn's name, just like I did to you." Woody reassures Edward.

Edward asks, "I'm not sure about this. Can you call Acorn first?"

Woody nods and says, "Okay, I will."

After hanging up with Edward, Woody turns his attention to calling Acorn. However, Acorn doesn't have any hands or feet to tap with. Instead, Acorn's unique way of answering calls by wiggling his nose, which soon starts to sneeze. "Achoo, achoo, and achoo, achoo, and achoo."

Finally, Acorn is able to respond, his voice is filled with curiosity. "Hello, who's calling?"

This is Woody here," Woody begins of his voice with a warmth sound, "I'm calling you about a fox carving named Edward, a new addition to Rozelle Park."

With the genuine delight, Acorn asks, "I see you made it back to your parent tree okay. But why are you calling me?"

Woody explains, "Well, Edward is rather shy, and he doesn't know anyone around here. Doodle is staying with Peaches for now, so it's just me and our parent tree to keep him company." He adds, "So, would it be alright for him to call you?"

Acorn agrees readily, "Yes, of course, he can call anytime."

Woody hangs up and instructs Edward by calling Acorn, "Now, give it a chance, make a call to Acorn." Then he adds, "Just remember to think 'Acorn,' and you will connect to him. Don't ask me how it all works; I haven't got a clue about this system!"

Edward asserts that he will give it a shot, as he has a newfound determination. He hangs up Woody and then he begins to concentrate on reaching out to Acorn, Thinking his name, "Acorn."

Acorn's unique response soon follows as his nose wiggles and goes, "Achoo, Achoo, Achoo." This continues on for a multiple times before he finally responds, "Hello."

Edward clears his throat, feeling with a mix excitement and curiosity. "This is Edward. I understand that you are called Acorn and are you in charge around here!"

"No, I'm just a messenger for my parent tree, the Old Oak Tree," Acorn explains humbly. "On my left is a carving called Hand; he only gives hand signals and carries a pocket watch with an alarm set for the time that you must return to your post, which is your den."

Edward listens attentively, then inquires, "What can I do around these parts?"

Acorn considers for a moment before he responds, "Well, you may be able to serve as a courier for your parent tree." And he adds, "I'll need to ask your parent tree about your new role, and Woody could also send messages through Rozelle Park, that if he's okay by him."

Edward then presents another question, "How can I contact my parent tree?" And he adds, "I don't know my parent tree's name; But I need to find out!"

Acorn provides an intriguing explanation, "It goes by E.S.P, which will help you communicate throughout Rozelle Park. Just call your parent tree 'Boss.' And the tree will answer."

Edward nods with the understanding and says, "I will do that." With a sense of newfound knowledge, he hangs up, unaware of the magical mysteries that awaits him in Rozelle Park.

E.S.P, or Extra-Sensory Perception, is a term often met with scepticism in the fields of psychology and wider science. It is considered an alleged paranormal or supernatural phenomenon, often portrayed in science fiction films. E.S.P encompasses of information or energy transfers, including phenomena like telepathy.

Despite the recent scientific understanding, surveys consistently demonstrate that the belief in E.S.P is remarkably widespread. Many individuals assert that they have personally experienced E.S.P, challenging the boundaries of what conventional science can be argued. The enigmatic world of E.S.P continues to be a subject of fascination and debate, blurring the lines between the known and the unexplained.

Edward places his paws on the tree trunk and thinks, "Hello Boss."

With surprise, Hazel responds, "Yes, Edward."

Edward, taken aback, asks, "How did you know my name?"

Hazell explains, "Through telepathy, I'm able to read your thoughts, and my name is Hazell."

She reveals her purpose, "I'm recruiting someone to act as my courier on my behalf, and I choose you."

Edward questions, "Why me?"

Hazell responds confidently, "You won't believe this, but through telepathy, I'll give you a call. You have the powers of E.S.P, which I find incredibly useful."

Feeling overwhelmed, Edward admits, "This is a lot to take in right now. Can I rest and speak to you tomorrow?"

Hazell reassures him, "Of course, you can."

Edward hangs up and he retreats into sleep, his mind abuzz with newfound knowledge and responsibilities.

The reason Hazel Tree chooses Woody to carry message across Rozelle Park is rooted in history. During the First World War, carrier Pigeons played a vital role as an extremely reliable method of sending messages. Over a hundred thousand Pigeons were used in the war, boasting an astounding success rate of ninety-five percent in delivering their messages to their intended destinations. These birds flew swiftly and the tanks like Wee Willy, the crew members also carried Pigeons to post messages about their whereabouts and the outcome of their missions, highlighting the trust placed in these feathered messengers during critical times. Woody calls Hazel, who responds promptly, "Yes, Woody."

Excitedly, Woody shares, "I've found a gold ring with a heart-shaped ruby surrounded by diamonds."

Hazell replies with a knowing tone, "Let me guess, you're hidden the ring in Doodle's Dray?"

Woody is astonished, "How did you know that?"

Hazell reminds him, "You already know I can read minds." She then offers her permission, "Would you like me to give you permission to show Edwards the ropes?"

Woody agrees, "The answer is yes; I'm the only one who can do this."

Hazell reassures him, "I don't think Doodle is coming back for a little while. Right now, he has much on his plate with Peaches."

Woody chuckles nervously, calls Edward, and his paws start to tap, tap, tap. "Oh my God, good luck with that, Edward. Hazell's reading my thoughts all the time."

Edwards replies, "Thank you. This will be noted! Well, I'm sleepy now, Goodnight." As he drifts off to sleep.

As the rest of the Hazell Tree inhabitants turn in and fall into their slumber. The Troops on both sides, returned to their post. However, before Major Tom and Nurse Glady's returned their post, they sat down on a park bench near the Wee Loch and began to converse.

Nurse Glady's opens up, "Major, I guess we used be an item in our previous lives."

Major Tom shares his own memories, "Funny you said that. When I read my orders for going over the top, I only remembered the day I died. But as time goes on and the longer my soul resides in this trunk, more memories come back. The memories show that I was married to you, and we had a child named Dennis."

Nurse Glady's reflects, "we were. We must return to our post now. We can discuss it tomorrow."

Major Tom agrees, "We must. Goodnight, darling."

Nurse Glady's replies with affection, "Goodnight, love."

In the mystical world of Rozelle Park, Edward, guided by Woody and Hazell, discovers the power of E.S.P and becomes Hazell's Messager. Meanwhile the echoes of past lives stir emotions among Major Tom and Nurse Glady's. Rozelle Park's inhabitants unite, their mission accomplished, as they continue their enchanted existence.

Chapter 11:

Enchanted Dawn.

Whispers of Magic in Rozelle Park.

As the following morning unfolds, Rozelle Park awakens beneath a breathtakingly sunny sky, not a single cloud to mar the perfection of the day. Peaches, fills with an inexplicable sense of wonder, gently nudges her still-slumbering companion, Doodle. "Wake up, Doodle! Wake up! She calls out, she shivers with a hint of enchantment.

Doodle stirs, with his eyes observing Peaches, and he murmurs, "Good morning, darling. This morning, you are truly radiant. What time did you arrive last night? I drifted off while I was waiting for your return."

Peaches replies, her words carrying a soft, ethereal quality, "It was incredibly late, my dear. Hand's watch pointed to11 30 pm. I couldn't bear to disturb your peaceful slumber; instead, I nestled beside you and let dreams carry me away."

Doodle inquires, his voice carrying a whimsical tone, "How did the night fare?"

Peaches' eyes twinkle as she responds, "It was a night of wonders! Robin and his feathery friends orchestrated a symphony that silenced the Germans, and Major Tom led his troops with a majestic grace. The birds, once our saviours, now find their roles fulfilled, and we are free to embrace our destiny." Her voice swells with an otherworldly excitement as she adds, "Doodle, I yearn for kittens!"

Doodle, the wise and patient, gently reminds her, "You are but a fledgling, not yet a year old, and the season for magic is in the heart of winter, when spring's breath awakens new life. No matter my efforts, the time has not yet come. Some older females may have embarked on this enchanting journey, but they have danced through more seasons than you." In the enchanted realm of the forest, the Squirrels have decided to take a moment of respite.

Over in the realm of the Robins, the Hatchlings, their voices a chorus of longing, call out, "Feed me, feed me! We are hungry, dear parents!"

Robina turns to Robin, her eyes gleaming with mystical curiosity, and asks, "Darling, how did the nights' tapestry unfold?"

Robin, the beloved leader of their feathered community, responds with a regal voice, "It was a night of grandeur! Major Tom assumed his rightful command, and we, the House Martins and I, woven spells that subdued the Germans. As I soared to meet Major Tom, I informed him that tranquillity had returned. He decreed that Peaches and the House Martins had fulfilled their roles and bade us to our realm."

Robina's gaze holds a glint of enchantment as she says, "This news fills our hearts with delight, my love."

Robin suggests, "We should take a journey to the abode of the House Martins, situated by the cottage outside of Rozelle Park. We will share our morsels of magic with our babes along the way."

Robina, her heart brimming with wonder, agrees, "An enchanting notion, my dear. Come, little ones, come with us." The Hatchlings' chorus of needs continues, "Feed us, dear parents!"

Robina sighs with a hint of mystical exasperation, "Ah, the demands of magical brood." The Robins take flight, their wings shimmering with the secrets of the woods, heading towards the domain of the House Martins.

A diligent provider in this realm of wonder, scours the enchanted earth for insects to nourish his family. Martina, guardian of their mystical nest, inspects her precious chicks, relieved that no misfortune has befallen them during the night. She beholds the first hints of feathers, a sign of the enchanting transformation to come, and whispers with a glimmer of prophecy, "My darlings are destined for greatness, and soon, I shall bestow upon them names. Martin will surely rejoice."

As Martin returns, he sees his beloved Martina radiating a mystical glow and remarks, "You shine with enchantment today, my love."

Martina, her beak curved in an otherworldly smile, replies, "Indeed, our chicks are adorned with budding feathers. It won't be long before I can join you in our magical quest for insects."

The Robins reach the enchanting Cottage, and their eyes fall upon the nest of the Martins. Robina greets them with an aura of magic, saying, "Greetings, Martins, how does the enchantment of this day find you?"

Martina responds with her own aura of enchantment, "We thrive, and our chicks blossom with each with each passing moment. Soon, I shall depart my nest and join Martin in our mystical dance among the insects."

The Robins, their hearts aglow with the magic of the Woods, depart, leaving behind an aura of wonder and possibility in their wake.

Chapter 12:

Reunion in the Enchanting Wood.

Rozelle Park's Mystical Embrace.

An Owl glides past Martin's nest, swiftly moving to the cottage roof. She dives into a hole in the chimney, entering the barn area of the cottage, and perches on a shelf alongside the chimney stack. This place was shared by her beloved partner, Barney. However, one day Barney ventures out to find food for their family and never returns. Her heart is filled with sorrows, and her memories are all that she has. With her Owlets being taken care of, she tries her best to provide for them without sacrificing too much. One day, as she embarks on a hunting expedition, the Rats seize the opportunity and make a devastating visit. When she returns, her heart shatters as she discovers her babies have disappeared. She is now left alone and also aging, unable to find another partner. She experiences great sadness and a longs for Barney's presence.

Robin notices the Owl, and asks, "Martin, I'm going to find out where that Owl went." He observes, "She looks unhappy." With determination evident in his movements, he instructs, "Take care of my family for now."

Martin nods in agreement, "Okay." He watches as Robin takes flight into the sky.

Robin soars up to the cottage roof, descends through the chimney opening, and enters the barn. He discovers Lily Bet, tears streaming down her feathers. He lands gently beside her, his wing extending to offer comfort.

Robin notices her distressed state. With genuine concern in his voice, he asks, "What's the matter?" And he adds, "Why are you so upset?"

Lily Bet's voice quivers as she responds, "I've lost my partner, Barney." She also adds, with a tinge of sadness, "I tried my best to raise our Owlets, but we were on my last brood." Her eyes well up with tears as she continues, "While I was hunting, the rats took them." The weight of the situation evident in her voice, she adds, "I'm too old to find another partner. What can I do?" As Lily Bet speaks, her feathers ruffle, reflecting her emotional turmoil.

"I'm Robin." He introduces himself, gently brushing his wing against her to try and soothe her. "Do you know of an oak tree with carvings and statues, topped by an owl?"

Lily Bet nods, tears still glistering in her eyes. "Yes, I do." And then she give her name, "I'm Lily Bet."

"Good to hear that!" Robin says with determination in his movements. He then adds, "I want you to go to the Old Oak Tree tonight around 8 20." Pointing towards the direction of the Old Oak Tree, he continues, "It might help you, to bring back some cheer in your life."

Lily Bet questions, "Do you really think this will help and cheer me up?" She cocks her head, seeking reassurance.

Robin's eyes gleam with hope as he speaks about Rozelle Park, describing, "It as a mystical and magical place." He invites Lily, to experience it herself and asks, "Can you come?"

After a moment's contemplation, Lily Bet nods. "Oh well, I'll go. I've got nothing else to do except hunt for myself."

"Good, I'll see you there," Robin replies with a warm supportive wing squeezes her.

As the day goes on and fatigue sets in, Lily Bet starts to Yawn. "Oh well, I might get some sleep now, Good day."

Meanwhile, Robin decides to spend the rest of the day with the Martins, catching up on the latest news and tales. He later discusses his plans with his partner, Robina.

"Darling, we can stay the rest of the day and have a chat with the Martins. When we get back tonight, can you stay with our little ones and put them to bed? I have another task tonight---to meet Lily Bet at the Old Oak Tree at 8 20." Robin explains, his wings slightly drooping with anticipation.

Robina, although annoyed, eventually relents, her movements reflecting her reluctant agreement. "This is the last time I'll let you go. But promise me, you come straight home."

"I won't be long, darling. It will only, take a few minutes." Robin assures her, his eyes filled with sincerity.

Martin chimes in with excitement, "Can I come too?" His feathers ruffle with eagerness.

"Of course, you can, "Robin replies, with his wings signalling for an invitation.

As the day turns into night, and the sun dips below the horizon, Lily Bet arrives at the Old Oak Tree. She lands gracefully beside a carving of an owl, unaware that it is Barney. A couple of minutes later, Robin and Martin arrive and settle in beside Lily Bet.

Lily Bet can't contain her curiosity any longer. "Well, I'm here now." And she adds, "What do you want from me?" Her eyes reflect a mixture of anticipation and trepidation.

"In just a few moments," Robin replies with a mysterious gleam in his eye, "You'll see Hand over there. He has a pocket watch in his palm, set for 8 30. It sends vibrations across Rozelle Park, and the statues and carvings will come to life. Just you wait." His wings flutter with excitement, echoing the anticipation in the air.

At precisely 8 30, Hand's pocket watch alarm emits vibrations and ripples through the heart of Rozelle Park. As the magical energy spreads, the statues and carvings come to life, waking up from their slumber. Among the first to stir is Barney, who begins to call out with his signature, "T wit, T woos, T wit, T woos." While his eyes glow a brilliant shade of green with his head turning first, to the left, then to the right by rotating 360 degrees, casting a remarkable spell on all those, who witness it.

Lily Bet, sitting nearby, can hardly believe her eyes and ears. The wooden carving of an Owl has come to life and is addressing her. She blinks in disbelief and then manages to utter, "Barney?"

Barney's wooden frame seems to shimmer with delight as he exclaims, "Lily Bet, is that you?" He then shouts, "It's me, Barney!"

Lily Bet, overwhelmed with her emotions, suddenly turns her eyes towards Robin. Her voice trembles with anger and sorrow as she shouts, "How could you!" Her heartbroken cry fills the air as she continues, "You made it worse, now I know he's passed on!" She takes flight toward the cottage, her feathers ruffled in distress.

Desperation grips Barney as he cries out, "Wait for me! It's me! It's Barney! Wait!" He detaches himself from his perch with a burst of newfound energy. His wings flutter with grace as they generate lift, propelling him forward. He's determined to catch up Lily Bet, his movements filled with purpose and urgency.

Meanwhile, Acorn the face of the wise Old Oak Tree, communicates with Hazell, another guardian of Rozelle Park. "Can you send Woody and Edward to summon the troops for a meeting by the Old Oak Tree?" Acorn's telepathic message resonates through the roots, reaching trees and their guardians.

Hazell responds with a sense of duty, "Will do! Acorn." She turns to Woody and Edward, giving them orders, "Your task tonight is to gather the troops and summon them to the Old Oak Tree for a meeting."

Woody nods, affirming his mission. "OK, I'll visit the Germans first," he says with a determine expression.

Edward, eager to assist, asks for guidance, "How can I find others, and which direction must I go to locate the troops?"

Woody offers a reassuring response, "Follow the trail on your left; you'll find Major Tom's Troops first and also this trail will lead you to the Old Oak Tree." His confident movements and reassuring tone convey a sense of purpose and readiness.

Edward nods in understanding, his steps infused with determination. "Alright then, I'll be off." He says, as he sets out on his mission. The magic of Rozelle Park guiding his way, filling the air with a sense of wonder and possibility. Edward's resolve grows stronger with each step, as he follows the trail on his towards Major Tom's Troops and the Old Oak Tree.

Barney finally catches up with Lily Bet and grasp her right claw, gently pulling her down to the ground. He holds her firmly but tenderly, his movements a blend of strength and compassion. He implores, "Please return to the Old Oak Tree, and I shall explain everything."

They return back to Barney's perch, landing grace fully. He proceeds to tell her his story, his voice fills with a mixture of nostalgia and longing. "I was thirteen years old when I passed over, my time had come. You, Lily Bet, are now twelve years old. We were fortunate enough to live a long and fulfilling life together." His eyes, though wooden, seem to glisten with emotion.

Lily Bet listens intently, her eyes reflecting a mix of sorrow and fond remembrance. She recalls their times together, the shared joys and sorrows. "We mated from our first season," she says with a hint of a smile, "and we did this for eleven years. Sometimes we had eleven owlets, and sometimes only three. The last we had... they were Monkey Face, Ghost, Church, Echo, and Hobby." Her feathers ruffles, and her movements reveal a deep sense of connection to their shared history.

Barney's heart swells with affection as he hears Lily Bet recall their owlets' names. He answers, "Yes, that's right. Now, what's going to happen with us?" His eyes convey a sense of hope and longing.

In the meantime, Acorn is overjoyed that Lily Bet has found Barney in the afterlife, and she hasn't crossed over yet. There's a sense of unity and hope in the Rozelle Park magic of weaving its enchantment.

Robin, watching from a distance, is satisfied that everything has turned out alright in the end. Pleased with the outcome. He and Martin take to the skies, their movements graceful and light, as they flies back home to their nest. As they soar through the air, they leave behind the awakened Statues and Carvings, who now to embrace their newfound life. The enduring mysteries and emotions intertwine, creating a tapestry of wonder and possibility within Rozelle Park.

Chapter 13:

The Summons to the Old Oak Tree.

Journeying Through Memories and Mysteries.

Hauptmann Clink strains to recall his family, yet all that surfaces is his time on the western front. Nevertheless, a flicker of memory emerges-the name of the town in which he was born. He thinks to himself, "Sins Heim! Sins Heim! If I can grasp that place, perhaps I'll a path to my loved ones." As his thoughts unfurl, his comrades begin to recollect their own origins.

Lancer Schneider chimes in, "I can recollect the town of Baumholder, where I spent my youth."

Sergeant Schultz adds, "Baumholder! Intriguing. It's coming back to me now." And he goes on, "I lived just outside of Kaiserslautern."

As the German wooden soldiers reminisce about their hometowns, they delve into the details of their origins. Hauptmann Clink's hometown of Sins Heim unfolds as a charming town nestled in the southwest of Germany, within the state of Baden-Württemberg. It lies approximately 22 Kilometres from the vibrant city Heidelberg and some 28 Kilometres from Heilbronn in the district of Rhein-Neckar.

Sergeant Schultz hails from Kaiserslautern, a city situated in the southwest of Germany, resting at the northern edge of the Palatinate Forest. This historic city finds its place in the State of Rhineland-Palatine, approximately 107 Kilometres away from Frankfurt am Main.

Meanwhile, Lancer Schneider proudly calls Baumholder his hometown nestled in the Birkenfeld District within Rhine-Palatinate, Germany. It resides in the Wistrich area, an historical region that spans across both Germany and France. Baumholder serves as the administrative centre and is renowned for its recognition as a state tourism destination and as a central hub for resorts according to state planning.

"I'm going to miss Christmas; it was my favourite time of the year," Sergeant Schultz laments, his voice choked with emotion.

Lancer Schneider adds with a heavy heart, "Me too."

Their moment of reflection is interrupted as Woody, a flying wooden pigeon, gracefully swoops down to the scene. Apologising for the interruption, he informs them, "I'm sorry, but I must break this up. The three of you have been summoned to the Old Oak Tree for tonight's meeting."

"And where is that?" inquires Hauptmann Clink with curiosity.

Woody responds, "The other side of the Wee Loch."

A sense of urgency fills the air, as Sergeant Schultz asks, "How do, we get there?"

Woody answers, "Just follow this track; it doesn't matter which direction you take. It's about the same distance, and you'll spot the Old Oak Tree. Look for an owl perched on top, its green eyes shining brightly, and listen to its soft 'T wit, T woos' calls."

As Hauptmann Clink and his men make their way in precise formation, following his commands with discipline and precision. The sound of their Jack Boots echoes as they turn to the right and march forward with quick pace. Their synchronised footsteps create a rhythmic cadence as they continue their march towards their destination.

Meanwhile, as Hauptmann Clink's men marches, Sergeant Schultz's thoughts drift towards Christmas, and he begins to hum the soothing melody of "Silent Night."

Silent night, holy night,

All is calm, and all is bright.

Round yon Virgin Mother and Child,

Holy infant so tender and mild.

Sleep in heavenly peace,

Sleep in heavenly peace.

Woody leaves the Germans to their march and takes flight, determined to locate Flight Sergeant Mitchell.

Chapter 14:

The Call of the Old Oak Tree.

The Wooden Troops Unites.

Edward, the wooden Fox, continues to move silently along the track, observing Gunner Lewis and Wee Willy engages in conversation. Gunner Lewis seems astonished as he exclaims, "I can't believe it, eight of you are inside that thing!" It appears that Gunner Lewis was referring to a vehicle that contained a surprising number of occupants.

The Tank Commander from Wee Willy nods, introducing the members of the tank, "Indeed. I'm Sergeant Jones, the Tank Commander and Brakeman. This is Corporal Smith, our Driver. 'HI.' He introduces Lance Corporal Thomas, the Left Gear Man, says, 'Alright, sport.' Lance Corporal Andrews, the Right Gear Man, adds cheerfully, 'Hi yah!' Forward Gunner Stewart inquires, 'Are you okay Pal!' Forward Gunner Dow greets with a friendly 'Hello.' Rear Gunner Smythe replies, 'What's up?' And Rear Gunner Brown reassures, 'Are you alright mate!'"

Gunner Lewis is curious about the nationalities of the individuals in Wee Willy's group and asks, "Who's the Ozzie, and who's the Yank?" Lance Corporal Thomas is quick to respond, proudly claiming his nationality, "Good day, sport. That would be me, The Ozzie."

Gunner Smythe, introducing himself with a nod, "Sup, Man. I'm the Yank, Gunner Smythe." It seems like Lance Corporal Thomas represents Australia, while Gunner Smythe identifies himself as an American.

Edward, the Wooden Fox, arrives on the scene and addresses them, "Sorry to break this up. You've been summoned by the Old Oak Tree." He instructs them, "I'm heading that way, you all can follow me, if you like."

In Unison, Wee Willy's crew asks, "Why have we all, been invited?"

Edward explains, "I don't know. I just received a message from my parent tree Hazell. She says, 'The Old Oak Tree has summoned all the troops in Rozelle Park for a meeting.'"

Gunner Lewis takes charge, his voice filled with determination and excitement, as he rallies Wee Willy, "Alright, men!" He gestures with authority, commanding their attention. He then turns to Wee Willy and asks, "let's form a unified file and follow Edward to the Old Oak Tree."

Edward asks, "Can I give the command?"

Gunner Smythe from Wee Willy responds, a hint of playful sarcasm in his voice, "Knock yourself out, Edward."

Edwards orders, "By the Right, Numbers!"

Wee Willy starts, "1, 2, 3, 4, 5, 6, 7, 8!"

Gunner Lewis chimes in with the final number, "9, Sir!"

In a confident and synchronised manner, showing their teamwork and coordination.

With precise timing, Edward commands, "Turn to the left," creating a moment of anticipation in the air. The men, Gunner Lewis, and Wee Willy, wait for the order with determination. As soon as the command given, Gunner Lewis takes the lead and executes a strong leftward pivot and stamping his Right Foot with confidence. Wee Willy follows suit, mirroring Gunner Lewis's movements, and executes a smooth leftward pivot, highlighting their coordination and synchronisation. The team displays their discipline and skill in executing the command flawlessly.

Edward issues his command, "By the Right quick march!" The wooden tracks of Wee Willy churn as Edward's right paw paves the way, and Gunner Lewis right foot follows suit. The rhythmic clattering of the tank's wooden parts reverberates through the air as Wee Willy advances. The crew maintains their cadence, singing their marching song, their voices melding in harmony as they dutifully heed Edward's orders.

Germans to the Left,

Germans to the Right,

And Fire!

Rat-a-tat-a-tat,

Rat-a-tat-a-tat,

And rat-a-tat-a-tat,

Boom, Boom,

Boom, Boom,

And reload!

Meanwhile, high above the Wee Loch, Woody's wooden wings catch the breeze as he spots the downed Spitfire wooden frame with Flight Sergeant Mitchell sitting on top of the left wing. Woody glides directly towards him and says, "Hello there, the Old Oak Tree has invited you and the rest the troops for a meeting."

Fight Sergeant Mitchell nods, saying, "Okay, I'll do that."

Woody adds, "You'll continue on, by yourself, and I have to find Major Tom and Nurse Glady's to pass on this message." With that, Woody takes flight once more, leaving Flight Sergeant Mitchell to follow the path toward the Old Oak Tree.

Woody momentarily forgets about Sergeant Lee and Gunner Peterson, but Flight Sergeant Mitchell doesn't have to venture far. He spots the two soldier on his left, comes to a halt, and warmly greets them with a friendly "Hello," continuing the conversation, he says, "The Old Oak Tree have invited us down the bottom of this for a meeting. I'd appreciate it if you two could come with me."

Sergeant Lee readily agrees, saying, "Sure, Flight Sergeant, we'll follow you." And so, Flight Sergeant Mitchell, Sergeant Lee and Gunner Peterson embark together on their journey toward the Old Oak Tree, ready to heed its summons.

Chapter 15:

Whispers of the Old Oak Tree.

Destines of the Reunion Amidst Among the Shadows.

Major Tom and Nurse Glady's meet up on a park bench near the edge of the Wee Loch. The moon shimmers, reflecting its dance on the tranquil waters, while the trees sway gently, creating a soothing atmosphere.

Nurse Glady's gives Major Tom a tender kiss on his cheek and says, "About last night, do you remember? My memories are coming back, and we were an item, even married." She asks, "Do you have feelings for me?"

Major Tom looks into her eyes and nods with a warm smile, "I have feelings for you." With love in his heart, " Sometimes, when I see you. I can't help but wish to attach myself to you." He confesses, his voice filled with affection.

"What make you say that?" Nurse Glady's inquires, her curiosity piqued.

Major Tom smiles, appreciating Nurse Glady's. "I say that because you possess qualities that truly stand out. Your dedication to providing exceptional care to your patients is evident in everything you do. Your compassion and empathy shine through, making you a beacon of light for those in need. Your knowledge and expertise in the medical field are impressive and inspiring. You have a way of making everyone around you feel valued and supported. It's these qualities that make me say what I do, as they make you an exceptional Nurse and an extraordinary person."

Nurse Glady's, who hails from Ayr somewhere in Scotland, beginning to remember giving birth to a boy named Dennis, left him with her parents for safekeeping before volunteering to serve near the front line, listens attentively. Many women, representing all walks of life, had felt it their patriotic duty to do so during that time. Unbeknownst to her, the child was Major Tom's.

A great-grandson of the couple, now a tree surgeon, had meticulously carved Nurse Glady's from an old photograph of her in uniform. And yet, somehow, the couple were picking up strange vibes, as if the two tree carvings had absorbed their souls and come to life, bringing them back together in this remarkable twist of fate.

Woody spots the couple and gracefully descends, landing in front of them. He delivers the news with a hint of apology in his voice, saying, "I'm sorry, but I've got to break you two up." He gives the summons to them and says, "All the residents in Rozelle Park are invited to a meeting at the Old Oak Tree." He adds, "I'm heading that way. You can follow me."

Major Tom's frustration is evident as he retorts, "This is not the right time at the moment!" He explains,

"We're trying to sort out our lives!" He changes the subject and asks, "Where do we go from here?"

Woody empathises with Major Tom's frustration but remains resolute, "I understand, but the Old Oak Tree is the benefactor of Rozelle Park." He concludes, "We must go."

Their plans were disrupted, but Nurse Glady's reassures Major Tom, "Come on darling, if we must!" She adds, "We can talk about this later." She turns to Woody and says, "Lead the way!"

Woody nods, his eyes glimmering with determination, and he leads the way with moonlight casting an enchanting glow on their path. Each step they take brings them closer to the Old Oak Tree, a place where legends are born, and destinies intertwine. As they approach, a sense of anticipation fills the air, for they know that a meeting of great significance awaits them. In this mystical moment, they embrace on a journey that will forever change their lives. With hearts filled with hope and courage, they move forward, guided by the magic that surrounds them. And so, their story stills unfolds, painting a tale of bravery, love, and the power of dreams.

Chapter 16:

Rozelle Park's Resonance.

A New Beginning Awaits

As the Old Oak Tree awaits the arrival of Edward, Woody, and the rest of the troops. Barney and Lily Bet are perched atop the tree. The two owls, their luminous green eyes shining brightly, await the gathering with a sense of wisdom and anticipation.

Meanwhile, Peaches and Doodle, the squirrels, have left their dray are foraging for nuts nearby. Peaches inquires of Barney, "Is there anything new?"

Barney responds, "This is my old partner, Lily Bet. She found me with the help of Robin."

The creatures of this park have their own unique style, they are all part of this magical Rozelle Park, ready to play their roles of this magical tale.

As the troops begin to arrive, Woody is the first to land gracefully next to Barney and Lily Bet, perched atop the Old Oak Tree. The 3 benches around the tree offer the perfect vantage points for the gathering.

Major Tom and Nurse Glady's arrive hand in hand, taking their place on a nearby park bench is thoughtfully provided by the mystical park. Their presence radiates a sense of unity and love.

Flight Sergeant Mitchell, Sergeant Lee, and Gunner Peterson follow, by positioning themselves on one of the benches in front of the Old Oak Tree. Next to Major Tom, with his arm around Nurse Glady's who sits beside him.

Moments later, the crew of Wee Willy arrives, their marching song growing louder as they draw near. The troops, both British and Germans, have assembled beneath the Old Oak Tree, united by the mysterious summons, ready to hear what Acorn, the voice of the Old Oak Tree spirits, has to reveal.

Amid the growing anticipation, Edward, the wooden Fox, arrives with the British contingent. His wooden form blends seamlessly with Rozelle Park's mystical ambiance, and he takes his place among the troops. In the background, the rhythmic cadence of Wee Willy's marching song continues:

Germans to the left,

Germans to the right,

And Fire!

Rat-a-tat-a-tat,

Rat-a-tat-a-tat,

Boom, Boom,

Boom, Boom,

And reload!

The enchanting melody adds to the magical aura of Rozelle Park, setting the for the final chapter of this mystical tale.

Lefty Face opens up the meeting and introduces the audience to Acorn, the Old Oak Tree spokesperson: "I'm glad you all come to this meeting." He begins, addressing the assembled troops. "I'll introduce you to Acorn. He speaks on behalf of the Old Oak Tree."

Acorn starts to make a speech, his words resonating through the still night. "I'm not one for speeches." He admits with humility. "Old Oak Tree says thank you to you, birds-Robins, House Martins-and you, Woody." Acorn nods towards the flying wooden pigeon. "And not to mention the addition to Rozelle Park, Edward." He acknowledges.

Acorn continues, "Thanks for your tireless efforts in passing on the messages. The past couple of nights following the eclipse of the sun." He says, "The weird green lights flashed in Rozelle Park, guiding the wooden soldiers and animals who have passed on to the afterlife."

He directs his gratitude to Major Tom, for splendidly arranging the missions that impede the chaos that has taken hold of these grounds."

Acorn concludes his speech with a solemn message, "Now you can get on with your new lives and obey the rules, and you will be safe until the time comes when you pass on again."

The troops listen attentively, the Old Oak Tree spirit's words sinking in as they embrace the magical and mystical world of Rozelle Park.

Barney, the wise owl, turns to the residents of Rozelle Park, wooden and mystical alike, shout in unison, "Hip-Hip-Hip-Hooray, Hip-Hip-Hip-Hooray."

Hauptmann Clink, deep in thought, addresses Schultz, "I've been thinking about Christmas. Since we will be hibernating during winter, perhaps we could celebrate it a week before we go into hibernation.

Sergeant Schultz responds with genuine enthusiasm, "That's an innovative idea, Sir. A wonderful way to bring some warmth and cheer to our winter slumber." The notion of a festive celebration in the heart of Rozelle Park resonates with the troops, adding another layer of magic to their mystical world.

The Christmas truce of 1914 was a remarkable and heartwarming moment in the midst of the turmoil of World War 1. It's testament to the desire for peace, even in the darkest of times. Soldier from different sides came together to exchange greeting in games of Football. In the midst of the conflict, they found a brief respite from the horrors of war, united by the spirit of Christmas. It was a reminder that, no matter the circumstances, the yearning for peace and connection can transcend even the most dire situations.

Indeed, the Christmas truce of 1914 serves as a poignant reminder of the humanity that can shine through even during the darkest hours of conflict. It's a testament to the universal longing for peace, unity, and connection, no matter the circumstances.

Major Tom, sensing that the meeting has concluded, asks, "Are we done here?"

Acorn, the wise spokesperson of the Old Oak Tree, smiles warmly and replies, "Yes, you all can go on with your business and have a good new life."

The crew of Wee Willy expresses their gratitude, saying, "Thank you."

As the meeting disperses, Robin and Martin fly back to their nests, carrying with them the messages they've faithfully relayed. Their nests are now filled with the joyful tales of this remarkable gathering, and they can continue with their nesting season undisturbed.

The soldiers returns to their posts, each one organising their new lives, inspired by the sense of unity and purpose they've found beneath the Old Oak Tree.

Barney is delighted that Lily Bet found him, and he waits with anticipation for the day they will be reunited.

Edward and Woody make their way back to their parent tree, Hazell, ready to embrace the new lives that awaits them.

And now, as the story of Rozelle Park, Part 2, comes to a close, let Acorn, the Old Oak Tree spirit, narrate the ending with a sense of wonder and anticipation for what lies ahead in Part 3:

"As the troops and residents of Rozelle Park gathered beneath the Old Oak Tree, we witnessed the extraordinary events that unfolded in our mystical world. The metamorphosis and transformation of lost souls by the emerald mist that enveloped Rozelle Park have left an indelible mark on our realm.

But our story doesn't end here. Part 3 awaits, where new adventures and mysteries will unravel, and the magic and mysticism of Rozelle Park will continue to captive us all. Until then, let us embrace the unity and harmony we've discovered and carry it with us into the future."

With these words, Acorn sets the stage for the next chapter of this enchanting tale, leaving the residents of Rozelle Park and the readers alike eager to embark on the next mystical journey.

On the 11th of November.

We stand and pray.

Remembrance Day, for those who led the way.

Soldiers, brave in battles, their lives they gave.

To please the Generals of the nation's might.

They marched to War, in the darkest night.

The lost lives, the cost we can't forget.

In memories deep, their honour's debt is set.

Scarred tombs of the unknown soldier, they rest.

In silence, their sacrifice, we must attest.

Red Poppies on the battlefields, a sombre sight.

A Symbol of courage, in the darkest fight.

So, on this day, we remember, and we pray.

For those who gave their all, on that November Day.

In honour or the fallen, we stand tall.

Their bravery and sacrifice, we recall.

Stephen Nigel

10/11/2023

Printed in Great Britain
by Amazon